SLOP GOES THE SOUP

A NOISY WARTHOG WORD BOOK

Pamela Duncan Edwards

ILLUSTRATED BY
Henry Cole

Hyperion Books for Children
New York

Printed in Hong Kong

This book is set in 18-pt. Bookman OS.
The artwork for each picture was prepared using pen, colored pencils, and watercolor paint.

First Edition

1 3 5 7 9 10 8 6 4 2

Library of Congress Cataloging-in-Publication Data
Edwards, Pamela Duncan.
Slop goes the soup: a noisy warthog word book / Pamela Duncan Edwards ; illustrated by Henry Cole.
p.   cm.
Summary: When a warthog sneezes while carrying soup to the table, he begins an
onomatopoeic chain reaction that involves the whole family.
ISBN 0-7868-0469-6 (trade) — ISBN 0-7868-2411-5 (library)
[1. Warthog—Fiction. 2. Clumsiness—Fiction. 3. Sounds, Words for—Fiction.] I. Cole,
Henry, 1955–ill. II. Title.
PZ7.E26365 S1   2001
[E]—dc21   00-40708

Visit www.hyperionchildrensbooks.com

A-A-A-A-choo! goes the warthog.

SLoP
goes the soup.

SLITHER go the hooves.

Wobble goes the birdcage.

CRASH

goes Uncle Fred.

CLATTER goes the table.

WHOOSH goes the teddy bear.

PLoP goes the pudding.

Giggle!

SLURP go the tongues.

RATTLE goes the bucket.

SPLASH goes the water.

Swish goes the mop.

DING! DONG! goes the doorbell.

GULP

goes the soup.

Have you ever noticed that some words sound just like the noise they are describing? This is called *onomatopoeia* (ahn-uh-mah-tuh-pee-uh).

Which word would you use to make this sound?

A balloon bursting . . .

POP

CHOP

SLAM

A ball falling down some stairs . . .

BUBBLE

BUMPITY-BUMP

CRUNCH

Can you finish this story using some of the words on this page?

CLIP-CLOP, CLIP-CLOP, CLIP-CLOP, **a warthog was walking down the street . . .**

Now, YOU finish . . .

CREAK SLURP CRACKLE GROAN SWOOSH
BOOM SLOP SPLISH-SPLASH SNAP PLONK
PLOP DRIP PING SMASH GURGLE RUSTLE
CLICK CLANK TICK-TOCK PITTER-PATTER
SQUIRT TOOT-TOOT SWISH

If you like, you can use your own words. Just make sure they are "sound" words. Make your own list and write lots of stories.

HAVE FUN!